DOG in BOOTS

Paula Metcalf

OXFORD
UNIVERSITY PRESS

Philip has a new neighbour—Penelope.
She has kind eyes, a waggy tail, and the most BEAUTIFUL smile!

'Just to go for a
walk with her would
make me the happiest
dog in the world.'

But there is a *slight* problem.
While Penelope looks very tall . . .

. . . Philip is not!

In fact, his legs are so short his ears sweep the floor when he walks.

On his daily trip to the café with his best friend, Ralph, Philip admits his worries.

'How will Penelope ever love me? I'm too tiny to kiss her, even on tiptoes!'

On their way home, in the late afternoon sun, Philip sees something that makes his heart leap. And gives him a fantastic idea.

The next day, they try to work out how that might happen.

Without, it must be said,
a great deal of success . . .

Until finally . . .

'Hey, Ralph,
I think we're on
to something!'

Later, Philip makes his way to Penelope's. He holds his
head high, takes a deep breath and . . .

'Penelope!
There's something
I've been longing
to say . . .'

'SQUIRRELS!' booms a voice from under the tablecloth.

And before Philip has a chance to say another word,
he lurches away at breakneck *speed.*

When the chase is finally over,
Philip glares at his friend.

'Remind me NEVER to ask you for your help, ever again!' he snaps.

Later that night, Philip
cannot get a wink of sleep.

He loves Penelope SO much,
but what on earth must she
think of him now?

Suddenly his thoughts
are interrupted by the doorbell. Uh-oh . . . it's Ralph!
And even more troubling, it's Ralph with a plan!

'We're NOT giving up, Philip!
Penelope WILL love you.
Especially when she sees how
sweet you can be!'

Actually, the plan turns out to be rather fabulous—a message to Penelope on the side of Philip's house. It will be the first thing she sees when she opens her curtains in the morning!

Philip wakes up early and stares impatiently out of his window. He can't wait for his love to see what he has written.

Penelope you smell of roses
your eyes are like pools of chocolate
I AM MAD about you!

Eventually, Penelope's curtains swish open.

But her reaction is not what he expects!

To Philip's horror, tears
begin to roll down her nose.
PENELOPE IS CRYING!

All Philip wants to do is go and comfort Penelope.
But he cannot let her see how short he really is!
Desperate times call for desperate measures . . .

Ralph!
Help!

Ralph tells Philip to meet him at the shops. He has another AMAZING plan.

'Flowers!' exclaims Philip when he meets his friend.
    'This plan is good!'

Ralph shakes his
head. 'No, Philip,
not flowers

...BOOTS!

'Then all we'll need is a pot of glue and some newspaper.'

Soon, Philip understands.

'WOW! I can see for miles!

Ralph, you are a genius!'

Now Philip feels more than ready
to go and comfort his love.

Philip is wobbly on his new legs, so leans against Ralph for support.

Penelope points up at his house and replies, 'What do you expect?'

'Don't worry,' cries Ralph, 'I'll fix it!' And in a flash he's gone
to close the shutter, leaving Philip alone . . .

. . . alone and WOBBLY!

With as much grace as he can manage,
Philip heads home.

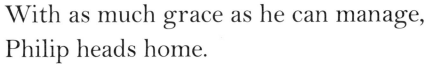

Poor Philip!
He is so upset he feels like he can never leave his house again!

But he should not cry! If only he would look out of his window, he would see something very unexpected—

Penelope smiling and wagging her tail!

And the reason Penelope is so happy?

Penelope has loved Philip since the first time she saw him through his window.

But he had looked so tall!

She thought she would never be able to kiss him, not even on tiptoes!

Penelope you smell of roses
your eyes are like pools of chocolate
I AM MAD about you!

Now she knows the truth!

KNOCK KNOCK!

Philip can't believe his eyes when he opens his door.

'I don't understand!' he gasps.

Over a cup of tea, Penelope explains herself. And then she asks Philip a very important question . . .

'Will you make me the happiest dog in the world and come for a walk with me?'

'I'd absolutely love to,' grins Philip . . .

And so they do.

For Maja, with love

OXFORD
UNIVERSITY PRESS

Great Clarendon Street, Oxford OX2 6DP
Oxford University Press is a department of the University of Oxford.
It furthers the University's objective of excellence in research, scholarship,
and education by publishing worldwide. Oxford is a registered trade mark
of Oxford University Press in the UK and in certain other countries

Text and Illustrations copyright © Paula Metcalf 2018

The moral rights of the author have been asserted

Database right Oxford University Press (maker)

First published in 2018

British Library Cataloguing in Publication Data

Data available

ISBN: 978-0-19-275884-2

1 3 5 7 9 10 8 6 4 2

Printed in China

Paper used in the production of this book is a natural,
recyclable product made from wood grown in sustainable forests.
The manufacturing process conforms to the environmental
regulations of the country of origin.

A note for grown-ups

Oxford Owl is a FREE and easy-to-use website packed with support and advice about everything to do with reading.

Informative videos

Hints, tips and fun activities

Top tips from top writers for reading with your child

Help with choosing picture books

For this expert advice and much, much more about how children learn to read and how to keep them reading ...